**Dr. Dewees**

# Consumption

# Anatiposi

**Dr. Dewees**

# Consumption

Reprint of the original.

1st Edition 2023   |   ISBN: 978-3-38230-162-0

Anatiposi Verlag is an imprint of Outlook Verlagsgesellschaft mbH.

Verlag (Publisher): Outlook Verlag GmbH, Zeilweg 44, 60439 Frankfurt, Deutschland
Vertretungsberechtigt (Authorized to represent): E. Roepke, Zeilweg 44, 60439 Frankfurt, Deutschland
Druck (Print): Books on Demand GmbH, In de Tarpen 42, 22848 Norderstedt, Deutschland

# CONSUMPTION.

## BY

## DR. DEWEES.

# PULMONARY CONSUMPTION,

## AND ITS TREATMENT

BY

# Inhalation of the Nutrient Elements

## OF THE BLOOD AND TISSUES,

AND

## SUPERFICIAL OR ENDERMIC APPLICATIONS.

BY

## H. P. DEWEES, M.D.

NEW YORK:

HALL, CLAYTON & CO., Printers, 46 Pine Street.

1859.

# PULMONARY CONSUMPTION.

THE blood from tuberculous subjects is found to be liable to certain alterations from the healthy state. The noticeable deviations consist chiefly in the imperfection of the elaboration of the fibrin; the decrease, in general, of the red corpuscles, and the increase of the so-called white or colorless corpuscles. Such defects must necessarily affect every process of nutrition.

Although every organ comes in for a share in this depreciated quality of the blood, yet the lungs, the mesenteric glands, and brain become the chief locations for the deposition of tubercles. They may invade by solitary deposits, or by disseminations through the tissues, with symptoms easily recognized in the plurality of cases; or, by a most insidious infiltration of one or both lungs, the only noticeable deviation from health being the gradual, but at first hardly perceptible, difficulty of breathing, or its increasing rapidity. Sometimes, while the congestion is accruing in the pulmonary cells, a deceptive disturbance in the functions of the stomach serves, for a time, to detract from suspicion of any error in the lungs.

Although the composition of tubercle varies under certain circumstances, it is found convenient, for practical purposes, to divide it into two conditions: the plastic and the aplastic. In the first we have the gelatiniform, semi-transparent, gray, miliary tubercle, possessing traces of abortive or degenerated organization; while in the second, or aplastic, no relics of organization are discoverable, the mass being what we know as the crude, yellow tubercle, granular, and disposed to soften.

The character of these tuberculous deposits depends on the condition of the blood, and the vital capacity of the tissues invaded. The plastic tubercle may degenerate into the lower grade of the aplastic, but the latter never advances into the former by any progressive change.

As above observed, infiltrated and also interstitial tubercle, is insidious in its derangement of the natural nutritive process of the lung tissue, the disintegrative deposits being of a microscopic character. They frequently escape detection during life, and even under post-mortem examinations, as the symptoms do not distinctly differ from those of sub-acute inflammation, unattended by tubercular depositions; whilst the pathological conditions are apt to be regarded, on common inspection, as the mere lymph products of the previous inflammatory actions.

In lungs which have been previously damaged, the state of the blood may assist in the corroboration as to their tuberculous depravity. Although inflammation of the lung may become the parent of tubercle, it does so only under certain conditions of the blood, already degenerated; or from disturbances in the *harmony of assimilative relation* in the tissues themselves. It is a fact to be remembered, however, that the *locale* of tubercle is not usually the seat of the preceding pneumonia, which more frequently attacks the middle and lower portions of the lungs, whilst tubercle chiefly invades the upper. When either the lungs or mesentery have been stealthily encroached on by tuberculous depositions, inflammation is prone to arise, and then the errors of the blood become manifested by rapidly-increasing deposits.

Although acute, or hasty consumption, is caused in a great measure by the rapid evolution of tubercles, and their consequent impairment of the function of the lung, yet this alone cannot serve entirely to account for the speedy waste and dissolution that melts, as it were, the lungs away in the profuse discharges, which in many cases so suddenly ensue, when the preceding cough was dry and irritative, or, at most, was accompanied by a frothy white-of-egg-like expectoration. Another condition arises, in the rapid decomposition of the nutrient fibrinous lymph into pus, by its contact with membranes whose integrity is insufficient for vital renewal, and which are fast verging of themselves towards disintegration and liquid dissolution. In these cases pus reproduces pus. The nutrient lymph exuded for the renewal of wasting tissue is in itself degenerated, and tends to further decomposition, whilst the organ to be nourished is degraded in its vital capacity; and thus lymph that should have been renewed, and tissue which should have been reproduced, mingle in the destructive changes that flood life away.

Even in these desperate states, arrest has sometimes taken place in an almost miraculous manner. A sudden change has ensued in the blood—the type of disorganization has been exhausted, and isolation of the degenerated portion commences. The exuded lymph becomes organizable, and a barrier to further destructive changes is established, by the production of a so-termed false membrane.

After the hepatization or consolidation of a certain portion of the lung has taken place, the retraction from the diseased condition may ensue quietly, provided the tubes remain open or become permeable, through which the expectoration can be voided. But certain blood changes must also ensue. Its fibrin, and other plastic components, must be more highly elaborated, that the new tissue shall be remodeled in proportion to the waste of the old. In such cases the restitution is comparatively perfect. In others no such remodeling or restitution ensues. The solidified lung has neither direct supply nor means of exit. The bronchial tubes are closed, although some loosened blood-clots may be expectorated; the air-cells are impermeable, and the decay of the impaired tissue is progressing. An abscess may be formed, and its contents may be evacuated by spontaneous softening and rupture, whilst a cavity, more or less extensive, is left. Sometimes, previous to the evacuation, and even softening of the diseased portion, the surrounding parts are relieved from their engorgement, and their air-cells again resume their functions. Organizable material may be thrown out, completely restricting the diseased parts, and rendering the discharge of the contained matter impossible, except through surgical means. If the abscess burst, lymph is exuded, and the cavity becomes lined with a membrane, which may secrete more or less  The patient may recover—not with a lung equal in volume to the natural condition, but with diminished capacity, as evidenced by the partial falling in of the walls of the chest. Sometimes the cavity-membrane secretes pus, with its gradual wasteful influence, or the cavity may not be completely lined, whilst the stealthy destruction of tissue keeps on. It may be slower or faster, but with noticeable loss to the sufferer. If perfect recovery take place, it is a mere matter of time, youth, climate, and increasing blood-purity.

In cases like these, we have a beautiful illustration of the *practical* differences between inflammation (which in reality is a disintegrating process, although by some miscalled "healthy,") and vitalization, which is the true power of repair. Upon the student this fact cannot be too strongly impressed—that inflammation is a perversion of true nutrition, whilst the highest type of development is in the perfection of vital action.

From the consideration of these views, the definition of what is meant by a strumous or scrofulous constitution can be readily gained; the amount of depravity varying with the state of the vital force existing in the blood, and in the structures themselves.

As a vast number of tissues enter into the composition of the body, they must necessarily depend on the blood for their reproduction. Yet it must be remembered that, although the blood contains the elements of renewal, yet the tissues must possess the vital power for organic selection and transformation. The same is seen in the growth of a plant. The earth contains the inorganic materials and the water, but the growth peculiar to it, and its proper principles, reside in the transforming power pre-existing in the early germ. Thus, two plants may be nourished from the same elements in the same mound, but their power of growth and transformation is self-inherent; one producing a poison baneful to animal life, whilst the other may afford its antidote, and a nourishment. In pathology the like holds good. The error may be in the blood, whereby every organ may be more or less attainted, or it may exist in the tissue itself, the blood being comparatively innocent, whereby growths or changes prejudicial to the well-being of the individual may be evolved.

A minute detail of the relation of the blood to the tissues and the various organic functions would be out of place here. But a cursory exposition may be necessary for the student, if not for the more advanced practitioner, that some of the various functions of assimilation may be comprehended. We will begin with the uses of the salivary secretion.

The saliva is secreted by the parotid, submaxillary, and sublingual glands, in conjunction with the follicles, distributed in and beneath the buccal mucous membrane. These follicles are very minute, and are surrounded by a plexus of capillary vessels. The peculiar substance upon which the salivary fluid depends for its converting properties is called "ptyalin." It acts as a ferment, and is chiefly furnished by the buccal glands. This organic constituent has a chemical action over the farinaceous elements of the food, converting the cooked starch matters into dextrin, or grape-sugar. Over the nitrogenized portions of the aliment it does not seem to possess any chemical reaction.

The gastric juice is secreted by the follicles of the stomach; its peculiar organic constituent, called "pepsin," in conjunction with the proper acid of the stomach, has the property of dissolving the animal or nitrogenized matters. This acid is generally supposed to be the hydrochloric. The gastric juice is not poured out during rest of the stomach. The presence of food, or other exciting substances, are requisite. The acid condition diminishes *pari passu* with the decrease of the contents of the stomach; the secretion becoming alkaline, or neutral, when the organ is empty. A moderate amount of stimulus, as produced by salt, pepper, &c., increases the secretion of the gastric juice; but, mechanical irritation, as induced by improper food, or by its excess, diminishes proportionately the secretion; a ropy, tenacious mucus being poured out instead. Frequently this is not the only evil. Nausea, with gagging or vomiting, is apt to ensue, whilst more or less bile may reflow or be pressed back through the pyloric orifice into the stomach, producing, by its power to arrest fermentative action, a train of evils only known to the rash dyspeptic. Vegetable acids, such as vinegar, lemon-juice, &c., at times have the power of retarding the secretion of gastric juice. The digestion becomes slower and more laborious. They become valuable remedies in those cases where the secretion appears to be too great. Ice, or very cold water, at first renders the gastric mucous membrane pallid, the secretion being retarded or completely arrested, until reaction is established, when a greater amount of gastric juice is secreted. Repetition of cold water may induce complete indigestion.

The quantity of gastric juice to be secreted depends more on the *demands* of the system than on the *amount* of food taken. This fact, although mentioned by authors, seems very little comprehended by non-medical persons. The portions of the food remaining unsaturated by the gastric fluid must either be refused by the stomach, or pass, in a crude state, into the duodenum, in an improper condition for further reduction. Duodenal dyspepsia is a consequence, attended with colic, spasm, diarrhœa, or disturbances in more remote parts of the system. This "overloading" is a frequent cause of convulsions, bilious febrile symptoms, &c., in children. Amongst those who masticate slowly and perfectly, this form of dyspepsia is rare; since time is given whereby the appetite is more readily satisfied, and the insalivation is rendered complete, by which the farinaceous substances are more easily converted into sugar, whilst the gastric juice is secreted in proportion to the demand. The stomachs of these "bolters" are subject to organic alterations, difficult of retracement even under a more prudent course.

The demands of the system on the stomach are greatly lessened from inactivity, and consequent loss of muscular tone, and from over-clothing; yet many persons of this description are habitually heavy eaters, and of course must be sufferers. They forget, or do not know, that a species of digestion has to be performed by every portion of the body. They continue with their inactivity, warm rooms, and over-amount of clothing; whilst the consequent feebleness operates against the actual requirements of the system for renewal. Hence, they become subjects for tumors, abscesses, tubercles, &c., as witnesses of their utter disregard to the necessities of their stomachs. How often do they exclaim, "At one time I could eat any quantity, and now am obliged to watch every mouthful!" Certainly, they not only could, but *did* eat any quantity. Pay-day must come, if the man lives long enough.

After a night's debauch, the thirst, the chip-dry mouth and throat, the rapid pulse, the feverish restlessness and bursting headache, are the mere tell-tales of the dishonored draft on the stomach for its "solvent," now more precious than gold. Any quantity of water is swallowed, but the gorging food remains undigested. The stomach becomes irritated, but will not secrete the evil-dispelling juice, and bile begins to be passed into the stomach, to increase the misery. Children are not the only ones that indicate by acrid secretions, aphthous patches, hives, and other skin eruptions, this over-cramming of the stomach; larger babies have the same.

Lesion or impairment of the functions of the pneumogastric nerves, tends to derange the digestive capability of the stomach. The secretion of gastric juice is not only impeded, but the stomach walls are impaired or deranged in their natural movements. Vomiting, inappetency, faintness, palpitation, spasmodic respiration, &c., form some of the attendants on this nervous derangement. In one case lately under my care, the amount of bile ejected was enormous, being accompanied by constant gagging and suffocative sensations. The gastric juice is the proper solvent for the azotized elements of the food, the starchy, oleaginous, and saccharine matters not being chemically acted on by it. The saliva, as before mentioned, presides in a great measure over the starch materials, the produced sugar being readily absorbed by the stomach. The uses of this product appear chiefly to support respiration, and to aid in the production of animal heat, whilst under certain circumstances it probably may be converted into fat. Fat is not a true histogenetic or fibre-making material, any more than other non-nitrogenized bodies. But the fatty matters, although not directly fibre-forming, yet enter largely into the formation of adipose and nervous tissue, and are essential in the acts of assimilation and in the reproduction of the early structures. The fatty materials are converted by the gastric juice into a more minute condition, or are held in suspension by it; whilst the albuminous matters are reduced by the aid of the acid of the stomach into a true solution, and into one uniform state.

The experiments of Bernard on solutions of albumen are highly interesting, and their results may lead to the better practical understanding of some of the forms of that Protean malady—Albuminuria, or Bright's disease. He found that a solution of albumen in very dilute hydrochloric acid, injected into the veins of an animal, made its exit speedily by the route of the kidneys; whilst a solution of albumen in gastric juice, so injected, left no discoverable trace in the urine. I am satisfied that in many of the cases of albuminous urine in pregnant women, and especially in the early stages, the acid of the stomach—now generally admitted to be the hydrochloric— being in excess, acts on the albuminous portions of the food as a ready solvent, and being rapidly absorbed into the vessels, the albumen is excreted by the kidneys, giving rise, like foreign matters thrown upon other organs, to congestion more or less extensive, and a disposition to those organic changes found to accompany albuminous kidney disease, of pregnant women especially. The lactic acid may also have the same solvent power over albumen. Although the derangements of the pelvic viscera happening with pregnant women—obstructive pressure upon the ureters, &c.—may accompany and aid this condition, yet they do not account for the whole attending phenomena. And sometimes, *in advance* of this albuminous showing of the urine, is puffiness of the face, or other portions of the body, followed by an erysipeloid affection of the skin, and even with indications of serous effusions into the cavities of the chest or cellular tissue of the legs.

Space is not allowed for the further mention of these views; but it would be well to caution certain " prompt" gentlemen of the profession, who hastily advise premature delivery, sacrificing the child, and many times injuring the mother, without fully comprehending the *causes* of the kidney derangement, and its frequent disappearance under properly-directed medical treatment. In further proof of these views, the albuminuria has often been seen to disappear suddenly, and coincidently with a change of the acid secretious of the stomach—in other words, spontaneously.

Not in pregnant women alone may this albuminous condition of the urine happen. It may ensue in the male, and in the unimpregnated female. In the tuberculous pregnant, it may serve to account for the arrest in the chest changes, independent of any other demand for the albumen of the blood. And *vice versa*, it may point out the cause of those cases in which tuberculosis has been dated from pregnancy, the albuminous excess of the blood producing depositions in the tissue of the lungs, independent of any kidney structural change. It is always prudent for the medical practitioner to remember, that some diseases are *complimental*, whilst others are *compensatory*.

Temperature has also a most important influence over the solvent power of the gastric juice. From 96° to 100° has been found most favorable. Amongst children, whose circulation is languid, where the temperature of the stomach is sufficient barely for digestive purposes, the "process of hardening" by exposure of their limbs, or by too light covering of other parts, not only aids in the reduction of the heat so essential to the stomach, but becomes the parent of scrofulous changes in the constitution, and also of tuberculous degeneration of the lungs.

Although for the most part we associate great bodily waste with pulmonary consumption, still it certainly does not attend in all cases. For we constantly see fatty, albuminous-looking people, whose lungs are greatly damaged, and who die from consumption, with a tolerably fair share of *embonpoint*. But they are weak, cannot undergo muscular exertion, and are terribly averse to fat in any shape in their diet—having their meats well done, and denuded of anything likely to produce it. So it is with those poor white-tissued, plump children, whose parents sacrifice them on the altar of prejudice or fashion. They think their children can stand it, as Mr. Smith's children have been so hardened—not noticing that Mr. Smith's children were fibre-producing, heat-generating little fellows, whose stomachs, perhaps, could afford it, or needed cooling for the degree necessary for healthful digestion.

There are other consumptives, from whom the subtle leech dissects every portion of fat; they can bear fatigue surprisingly; they cough day and night; they eat prodigiously, and bear fat well. Indeed, many seem to almost live on it. They fairly walk into their graves, which have so long been claiming their skeleton bodies. They die, after being housed only a few days, either from hæmorrhage, or because there was not sufficient lung surface left unconsumed, for the absolute atmospheric wants of the system. On examination of these defying cases, although the lungs are found excavated, yet the portions that are left are comparatively sound—the tubes are not occluded by infiltrations of matter, and the remaining cells are not thickened or changed in their normal structure—there were only not enough of them. I have seen such fight on, and get well; whilst others have fought on to the last, with the hope lingering that the victory would still be on their side.

Consumption, that is, tuberculous disease of the lungs, though in most cases attended with cough and profuse expectoration, is not always so—a person may have *dry* consumption—the cough being a mere irritative hack, or a long wheezing one, with a bronchitic expectoration, if any, like the white of egg. They gradually fail; no particular symptom records the cause; every function seems to decay with even step, whilst the lamp of life burns brightly on one or both cheeks —in some only put out by the heavy dewy sweats, to be relit on the morrow more brightly still. And thus, life " growing sanguine with its lightening load," and the voice becoming whisper-silent, they sink into that sleep whose dreams are undisturbed, and whose wakening is full of promise.

In my own experience, I have found a low gastric temperature attending those troublesome cases of regurgitation of the food, the particles being scarcely acted on, although they may have laid in the stomach for several hours. The persons so afflicted are apt to complain of having "cold stomachs;" but this condition of regurgitation may also happen when the stomach temperature is too high—the pieces rejected, however, are generally more or less softened. Diarrhœa is more frequent in its occurrence from this state, than regurgitation, owing to the irritation established from the passage of crudities into the duodenum.

The fatty matters, besides their disposition in the formation of the nerve vesicles, have a special destination in the primitive growth of other parts of the organization. They serve to maintain animal heat by combustion within the lungs. Even malignant growths demand fat as one of their elements. A due admixture of oleaginous substances appears to be absolutely necessary, not only for the digestion of the albuminous materials, but also for the growth of the tissues. It is probably owing to the neglect of this law that so small a proportion of true contractile muscular fibre is to be found in the fat, white-tissued-looking persons. The fat they possess is the product of conversion of the albumen, and the *vegetable* oil matters in the cells of the plants consumed. They lack fibrin—the very scaffolding necessary for fibre growth; and when attacked by tuberculous or scrofulous disorders, they melt down, as it were, without the power either of resisting waste, or of remodeling. Wounds, or any breach of continuity, heal in them with difficulty, and are only forced to do so, under artificial stimulus, constitutional or local, by which the fibrin may be engendered for constructive purposes. This class of persons are subject to consumption; and their cure, if it take place, can only be effected through those means which render the blood less albuminous and more fibrinous, by dietetic regimen and superficial remedial application. With these, albuminuria is not only incurrent, but I have seen it preservative; the kidneys acting as safety-valves in the withdrawal of the excess of albumen. They are also subject to ulcers of greater or less extent and number, that appear by their curdy discharges to run off the same excess of albumen, whilst by their irritation the fibrin is increased. Practically, it is not found beneficial to heal these ulcerations suddenly, as albuminuria may become established, if not present, or be increased if previously existing. The substitution of the animal oils, or cod-liver oil, in these cases, is not only difficult, but at times impossible. Indeed, in most of them, the fault does not lie in the oil matters, which, although imperfect, are abundant; it lies in the deficient elaboration of the plastic elements. We now see that consumption may depend not only on deficiency of the oleaginous materials, but also on the deficiency or depravity of some others; and the remedial selection is only to be made by the careful grouping of the symptoms, and by the analysis of the assimilative relations of the patient. The benefit accruing from the use of cod-liver oil in many wasting disorders, is mainly to be attributed to the importance of fatty matters in the process of assimilation.

The inorganic materials of the blood also serve important uses, in regulating its chemical condition, and in supplying the necessary bases of growth. The potash salts hold a special relation to muscular substance; the phosphates and carbonates of soda maintain the alkalinity of the blood; whilst the chloride of sodium, or common salt, renders important services, not only to the solids of the body, but also to the secretions. In the young growing tissues, in the formation of the skeleton, and the teeth, the phosphate of lime performs a most valuable office. We now see the *rationale* of the employment of the hypophosphites of lime and soda, recommended by Churchill in the treatment of consumption—they not only act as absorbents, but repair or retard the waste of tissue. In the blood, muscles, and hair, iron enters largely.

Every tissue is subject to disintegration. The equilibrium of the system is sustained, by the supply of new material—being in proportion to the waste. When the decomposition of the structures overbalances their renewal, the loss of flesh is alone attractive to the non-medical observer. But, to the physician, it becomes significant of an over-accumulation of carbonic acid in the system. The individual is gradually becoming more or less poisoned. For the removal of this carbonic acid, and for the renewal of the consumed oxygen, the lungs are the most efficient organs. In the delicate membrane of the air-cells these changes are effected. But, if superficial impediment, as from obstructive mucus or thickening of the membranes, and consequent diminution of the interior capacity of the cells ensues, the vital interchanges are interrupted, and the whole organism is made to suffer.

The liver, also, aids in the excretion of hydro-carbonaceous matter from the blood. But the bile is not altogether excrementitious, since part of it is destined to be re-absorbed for the further uses of the economy. It is easy to comprehend from this view, that the arrest of the secretion of bile, not only causes the delay in the blood, of the materials that should have made their exit through the liver; but also, that the portions which should be re-used for the purposes of assimilation, are not afforded. It behooves us to remember that the so-called in-activity of the liver may not be a sort of paralysis of the organ; but that the amount of materials forced upon it by an imprudent disregard to diet, are too great for its power to eliminate; and this, especially if the lungs are deficient in the acts of respiration.

The popular error of the bile "being something to be got rid of," has, no doubt, provoked many an assault upon the liver, by purga-tives and " alteratives," once so fashionable, whilst the so self-inflicted have sunk down, bewailing their misfortunes and their livers.

One of the peculiar offices of the bile, is to regulate through its al-kaline action, the *degree* of the acid products of digestion. When duly mixed with the ingested chyme, it prevents chemical changes in the reduced pulp, thereby restricting the too rapid evolution of gas from fermentative decomposition, so troublesome to the dyspeptic. When bile reflows into the stomach, it becomes a source of discomfort, by the power it possesses in retarding the fermentative actions proper to the early digestion. These cases are sometimes troublesome to treat.

Dyspepsia is commonly regarded as a disorder of the stomach alone. But the duodenum, the cœcum, and other portions of the intestinal tract, have their appropriate dyspepsia. The translation of their symptoms can only be made out by the observant practitioner. Too much food for the amount of bile secreted is as injurious as too much bile for the quantity of food. These "weak-livered" people, these windy complainers, these supper-nightmare-invoked dyspeptics, form a large class in society. They are particularly fond of changing their doctors, or of gulping down quack nostrums. The homœopathic glob-ules of moonshine are a Godsend to them. They can be continually taking these sugar nothings not only *without injury*, but with mental benefit. They change everything but their diet. Their skins become pasty yellow with a clammy sweat, or their palms burn whilst the sur-face is dry. The clothes begin to hang in festoons; their conversa-tions about their ailings are only interrupted by eructations, or abor-tive hiccups, whilst their bowels bag down in the protruded walls of the vein-covered abdomen. They are really unhappy in every fibre, and certainly are very uncomfortable companions.

Sometimes "chronic diarrhœa" is established; the bowel surfaces are irritated by the semi-digested acrid particles, producing constant propulsive efforts. The discharges are generally whitish, offensive, and mixed with portions of the food, but without bile, which in some cases may make its appearance at the close of the strainings. In others, there is an over-quantity of bile with each stool, whilst portions of the food may or may not be discoverable. By repeated irritation, the glands in the duodenum cease to secrete, or else secrete improperly, and thus aid to impair those changes so essential for the renewal of healthy blood. Sometimes constipation attends the withdrawal of biliary secretion, the whole intestinal tract being sluggish.

When the food has been properly emulsified by the combined actions of the bile, pancreatic and enteric juices, the resulting chyle is subjected to the actions of the lacteals or intestinal absorbents. After the absorption by the lacteals has taken place, the alimentary matters are submitted to the internal glandular actions, through which changes are effected to render them assimilable. The substances taken up by the vessels of the stomach and intestinal walls, are subjected to the direct actions of the liver through the portal circulation. Thus it is, that the liver becomes an organ for assimilation as well as for depuration.

The influence of these combined actions over the production of tubercular consumption, is now manifest. The nutrient materials brought by the lacteals, the mesenteric and gastro-intestinal vessels, have to receive certain vito-chemical metamorphoses, that in part prepare them for the purposes of the blood, before entering the general circulatory current.

It is during the passage of the albuminous portions of the chyle through the lacteals, that the incorporative admixture of the oleaginous matters ensues. From this point the perfectioning of the albuminous and fatty particles of the food into "cells," takes place, by which they are rendered capable of assimilation. Without these oleaginous materials, this vital act could not be sustained, and the various nutritive processes would become abortive. Fat has first to *enfilm* the nascent cell (whose function it is to bear life and regenesis into every portion of the body,) before nerve-vesicle or tissue can be fully developed. It is prompted by nature, that the inhabitant of cold climates shall partake of the gross fatty animal matters, whilst in the warm regions he still seeks those foods which shall yield saccharine matter, and the lighter vegetable oils. The process of enfilming must be carried on even in warm climates; but animal heat in these regions is more easily sustained, and only enough fat matter is required for cell growth, and the construction of the adipose, nervous, and muscular structures.

If the fatty material be imperfectly supplied for enfilmation; or if the due amount be not *properly incorporated in the cell*, the reproductive energy of the structures becomes weakened or perverted, whilst the door for tissue waste and tuberculous deposits, &c., is opened, and chemical actions, with decay, are unrestricted. The old maxim that "evil communications corrupt good manners" holds good here. Decay begets decay; so leavening the whole, that vital energy has no restrictive barrier against death claiming its victim.

We will now refer more particularly to the transformations observed in the chyle during the vital process of nutrition. During its passage through the mesenteric glands, the resemblance to the blood becomes more apparent by the increase of the fibrin. It is now that the chyle corpuscle is found to be enveloped in a delicate film of oil, whilst the fibrin of which it is chiefly composed progresses towards a higher degree of vitalization. The chyle ingredients exist in different relative proportions, according to their progress from the intestinal walls to the mesenteric glands, and from these to the thoracic duct, or the great channel to the heart for the tissue uses of the economy. The proportion of fat, or oil globules, in the chyle, when passing from the intestines to the mesenteric glands, is great, whilst the albumen is only in a noticeable quantity. The chyle still appears to be a mere emulsion. True chyle corpuscles are yet deficient, and the fibrin has not been evolved. In its passage from the mesenteric glands to the thoracic duct, however, certain distinct changes ensue. The oil globules decrease, albumen exists in its greatest quantity, with vast numbers of chyle corpuscles, though not fully developed. The fibrin is now

2

noticeable, whilst in the thoracic duct the fat in the chyle diminishes with the albumen, and the chyle corpuscles become well developed, and properly enfilmed with oil, with fibrin in great quantity.

It then becomes a matter of vital importance that the food should contain a proper proportion of saccharine, albuminous, and oily elements. Although the first two can be drawn from either vegetable or animal diet, yet the actions of these constituents in the blood differ materially, as seen in the disorders of gout and rheumatism. This difference is very noticeable in many consumptive patients, who, although requiring the due admixture of all the elements above mentioned, yet find by experience that it is not a matter of indifference whether they be supplied from animal or vegetable sources.

Since the conditions of the chyle, as above mentioned, vary greatly in the different elaborating portions of the system, it requires not only the patient's experience to discover what articles—vegetable or animal—disagree; but, also, the medical man's scientific investigations, to determine *why* they disagree. It is an every-day occurrence to find some consumptives not only averse to oleaginous matters, but with whom these matters are practically found to disagree. Some find that the albuminous constituents of animal food derange their digestions, and fail to nourish, whilst others refuse those from vegetable diet. Still, the principle remains the same—the chyle formations (including the lymph) must be healthfully sustained, that the blood products shall be normal. The generation or renewal of tissue cannot be maintained, without affording to the blood not only the elements necessary for its reproduction, but also the *quality that is in organic harmony* with the structures themselves.

There are many consumptives who, apparently, have never been troubled with dyspepsia; and there are many dyspeptics who have died free from tuberculous disease. Although this is true in some cases, yet it must be remembered, that dyspepsia is but too often regarded as a mere stomach disorder, attended with more or less inconvenience or local pain But dyspepsia has no exact regional boundaries. Its influence in producing or aiding tuberculous depositions is held within certain limits; the disorder so induced being an index of the blood changes resulting from the dyspepsia. The absence of any of the forms of dyspepsia, however, does not indicate any immunity from tubercle. Its deposition may result from *errors originating in the disturbed elective actions of the tissues themselves.* Tubercle may be thus evolved, and stored up.

Pulmonary consumption is regarded by many as a disease originating within the lungs themselves; but certainly by the profession it cannot be so viewed. The investigations of the blood tend to prove, that the practical starting-point of tuberculous disease of these organs lies in most cases in the imperfection of the digestive functions, and in the want of proper elaboration which the lymph and chyle undergo in the great laboratories of assimilation, viz.: the lacteals, mesenteric vessels and glands, and in the thoracic duct. The anterior disorders of the nervous system are not mentioned here, as they would lead into a discussion beyond our space.

Nor is consumption always to be set down to the ravages from tubercular deposit. We find many lungs on inspection full of cavities, and infiltrated with pus; from the *constitutional* exhaustion of which, death has supervened. Although this condition may be accompanied with tubercles, here and there scattered through the lung tissue, yet they were comparatively innocent of any highly deleterious influence. It is in these cases that pneumonia, or local inflammation of certain circumscribed portions of the lungs, becomes the parent of so much evil. The portions so deranged in their nutrition break rapidly down, attended more or less by hæmorrhage, and pus-like expectoration, if an exit can be found; or with abscesses of various sizes, if the tubes are occluded. The fever and irregular chills are more early prominent than in true tubercular phthisis, whilst the loss of flesh and strength is due more to the wasting of the lung, and its consequent imperfection in the respiratory changes that should have been afforded the blood, *whereby other organs are depreciated*, from want of proper arterialization, than from any depravity sustained by the blood. Organic blood changes no doubt do take place, but the few scattered tubercles indicate the amount not to have been very serious. It is only by perversion of the normal nutrition of the lungs (in those previously healthy) that pneumonia becomes the parent of gross tubercle. Nor is the seat of the tubercle always the immediate *locale* of the forerunning inflammation. It may be more or less distant.

In other instances, however, a tuberculous exudation seems to be established, and becomes the inciter of pneumonia. The air-cells become choked, and inflammation succeeds in circumscribed portions. These may be near the pleural boundaries, especially towards the upper region of the lungs, or deeper in its substance. When in the first position, pleurisy is of frequent occurrence, the pain persisting a given time, and changing with any subsequent pleuritic disturbance. The risk of perforation, with consequent emphysema of local points, or of making a communication between the bronchial tubes and the pleural cavity, is always to be regarded as contingent. Generally, lymph is exuded on the pleura, and that portion is bound to the ribs by tough bands, or is firmly glued to the opposing surface.

This exhibit of tuberculous material within the air-cells sometimes appears to be an effort of nature to discharge the offensive matter, and, as seen to result in other organs engaged in vicarious excretion, inflammation arises, with consecutive structural changes. But, generally, the blood does not seem to have suffered primarily; a pulmonary catarrh has become more or less chronic, perhaps incident from measles, small-pox, scarlet fever, or other eruptive disease, and attended with a profuse blennorrhagic expectoration, which gradually becomes inspissated into an albumino-fibrinous material, somewhat representing the granular deposit of sthenic pneumonia, and which, by gradual absorption or drying up of the more watery portions, leaves a soft, cheesy, tuberculous matter. This may be thrown off by degenerating into pus, without increasing renewal, and with returning soundness to the pulmonary tissue; or it may remain within the cells, undergoing further tuberculous addition and degradation, and by its accumulative pressure destroy their walls. In this latter persistence of infiltrative deposits, the blood has probably assumed tubercular genetic changes. Rheumatism, and disease of the heart, which induces bronchial engorgement, are frequent antecedents of this catarrhal tuberculous state, and especially if conjoined to a scrofulous or syphilitic taint, from which the sub-mucous tissues are prone to derangement.

In the young especially, chronicity may not attend—but one tumultuous attack, ushered in with acute pneumonia, may cause the patient to succumb. Not unfrequently, in the chronic cases, the intestinal mucous membrane evidences, by a catarrhal secretion, its participation with the pulmonary disorder.

These cases resemble, but in many points differ from what is commonly called scrofulous consumption, in which the blood itself is the chief source of the disease. The mode of attack is also different. For the most part, in scrofulous phthisis, the disease is hereditary; its antecedents are of long establishment; its incurrence can generally be predicted; its precursors are more or less stealthy, and its cure, if possible, is only to be effected through the blood. In the other form, there need be no scrofulous blood condition. It is spontaneous, and not traceable to any family transmission. Its antecedents for the most part are sudden, or irregular, and it can be traced to some known local cause, such as pneumonia from exposure, &c. Its incurrence is not predicable; and its cure or eradication by topical remedies is more readily effected; the scrofulosis of the blood (if any has been superinduced) being temporary, attributable and alterable; as in general the digestive system has been but little deranged, or is amenable to treatment.

Although pulmonary consumption, in the plurality of cases, appears dependent on the insufficiency or imperfection of the oleaginous elements afforded the blood, yet it cannot be denied that it ensues in many other instances, where the fatty matters are in due quantity at least. In some, fatty liver attends, and the depreciation of adipose substance in the body is not remarkable. The deficiency of sugar, however, is marked.

These cases seem to depend on the surcharging of the blood with albumen, its conversion into fat by the liver, and its averseness to the necessary metamorphosis into fibrin, by which the young growing tissues are afforded their basis of renewal. The lungs become more or less infiltrated with an albumino-tuberculous matter, whilst the true tissue degenerates, loses its normal character, liquefies into pus, or *becomes atrophied.* The expectoration consists of pus from the dissolved tissues, of the degenerated material of blasted renewal, and the softened tuberculous matter. The destruction of the lung is a steady process of disintegration. Persons affected with this form of consumption keep up a certain rotundity of outline, their muscles are weak and uncontractile, they are loosely put together, and in general they have a doughy look, although some retain their color in a most remarkable manner.

In the light or red haired, the superficial vessels of the integument and of the bronchial membranes are near the surface; they oxydize, as it were, more rapidly. Breaches of continuity easily take place; or rupture of vessels is easily induced by violent coughing or exertion. Hæmorrhage does not appear to injure, and in many it seems to afford relief. Being more sudden and profuse, the blood is apt to be thrown immediately off, the gravitation and the plugging up of the air-cells, by its clotting, being less frequent than in the dark-haired, torpid, and swarthy-complexioned. In these the *bronchial* tuberculous disturbance is greater. But the vessels do not lie so near the surface, and hæmorrhage is less frequent, whilst the nervous erythism is less active. As a general thing, they are more averse to cod-liver oil, or fat in any shape, preferring well-done meats, without gravies. The albuminous elements of the blood are not only defective in quality, but appear to be in too great quantity. The liver becomes fatty, with atrophy of its true tissue. This condition, however, belongs more to the general tuberculous dyscrasia, than to isolated pulmonary degradation. Fibrin is deficient for the purposes of re-formation of tissue.

We above stated, that fat possessed the property of rendering the digestion of the albuminous materials of the food more easy. But in the cases just cited, there is an over-introduction of albumen into the blood, and fat is instinctively avoided by the individual. The liver, it would seem, labored in the withdrawal of the excess of albumen, either by converting it into fat, or its proper tissue degenerates and atrophizes, whilst the albumino-fat is deposited, at the expense of its true tissue, and the sugar is reduced in quantity, for the combustion in the lung. The waste in these cases must be great, as the oxygen of the air consumes the tissue. Sometimes the conversion of albuminous compounds into excess of sugar (independent of its production from any other source) intervenes, and the kidneys are called on, producing the diabetic condition, so frequently found alternating, or coincidental with pulmonary tuberculous disease. At times the insipid form of diabetes may be owing to the derangement, or over-introduction of albuminous materials into the blood. It must not be forgotten, that these elements going to the liver, are not the *perfected* ones existing in the blood. Certain changes have to be effected, and the *integrity* of the functions of this important organ is essential, not merely in the necessary elimination of the bile, but in the *vitalizing* property afforded the albumen, which is the true *pabulum* of the tissues.

Two conditions, at least, are necessary for normal reproduction, viz.: 1st. Purity of the blood, containing the *pabulum* of the structures; and 2nd. Integrity of elective action in the tissues to be reconstructed. Hence, unsoundness of organs may arise from a depraved state of the blood; and on the other hand, the blood may be changed from the healthy condition, by derangements originating in an organ itself. In this latter manner, disease may be engrafted on other, or distant portions. the destructive tendency being measured by the vital importance of the part secondarily affected. The changes that a diseased organ forces upon the blood have not been sufficiently studied. The so-called complications are generally viewed as being dependent on the same conditions that originated the attack. But this is not always true, as these complications differ in their exhibition, when the parts so included receive a similar impress from the exciting cause. Every healthy organ has to withdraw from the blood the elements of its own structure. It is not to be supposed that the blood, after it has nourished the kidneys, for example, is in the same vito-chemical condition as after it has performed the same assimilative function in the brain. The *non-extraction*, then, or the *undue withdrawal*, from the blood of its elements must derange its composition, by interfering more or less with every functional process. In addition to this, the mal-secretions tend to engender further depravities. Of these facts the physician should never lose sight. The original disease, or disorder, is to be discovered first, and then treated; the functional complications will take care of themselves, or be of easy regulation. This metamorphosing of the retained elements, which should have been otherwise appropriated, is a frequent source of disease. Albuminuria, diabetes, fatty degeneration of organs, tuberculous encroachments, &c., &c., are instances of this want of organic equilibrium.

The derangements of the nerves of organic life—the mechanics of the body—come in for a large share in the production of. disease. There may be a morbid excess in the nervous action, by which more material is invited to the parts than can be worked off, producing interstitial hypertrophy,· or changes of the nutrient exudations into abnormal products, or into infiltrations, which pass through various grades of degeneration down to pus, may ensue, whilst the natural tissue undergoes the atrophic process. At other times, however, the so invited elements do not undergo any inferior metamorphosis, but they are co-modeled into true tissue, giving rise to "fibrillar hypertrophy," attended with exaggeration of function proper to the part.

This condition is seen in true fibrillar hypertrophy of the heart, where the impulse at the wrist, in many cases, fails to record the actual state of the system. The pulse is strong, may be frequent, from the increased irritability, whilst the general system is below par. The treatment, to be successful in these cases, must recognize these opposing states. Sedatives, topically applied, will serve to quell the heart's tumult, whilst tonics and nourishing diet are to be taken, to sustain the working powers of other organs, whose functions are essential to the life of the individual.

Lastly, a third condition may arise from these derangements of organic nerves. The normal tissue may be converted into false structure. It may be innocent as regards its influence; the disturbances created being more of impediment, than of vitiated function. Or, there may arise growths malignant to the surrounding parts and to life, the blood receiving those changes which are destructive to its integrity, and to the continued health of the different organs. The hypertrophies, dependent on dilated vascular supply, are sometimes consecutive to the increased organic nervous demand.

From these views, it would appear that consumption may be generated by errors of the nervous system, directly, or indirectly, affecting the harmonious co-relations of the blood and tissues. It certainly has followed from fright, from mental depression; from injuries embracing both, independent of any depravity that may arise from absorptions and disintegrating reactions of pus, or from obstructed nutrition, owing to the plugging up of the minute nutrient vessels by fibrin, or portions of detached fibrinous concretions, &c. How often has it followed grief, or unrequited love, or any unreconcilable disappointment, without apparent hindrance in its course of dissolution; unamenable to remedy, to change of climate, and apparently without much appreciable depravity of the blood! The moral causes being persistent, the changes resulting to the local nervous system are also persistent; and thus structural alterations and refusals go on. They who have endeavored " to minister to a mind diseased," know the difficulty.

Accompanying pulmonary phthisis, and aiding its rapidity and its exhaustive progress, comsumption of the bowels stands prominently forward. The tuberculous ulcers may attack the ileum and colon, or they may extend upward to the stomach. The mesenteric glands become more or less tuberculous, and in many instances amongst children, (especially among the mulattoes,) these and other abdominal glands are completely ravaged by tubercular deposits. Thick, viscid discharges ensue from the whole mucous intestinal tract, and the acute softening is so great and sudden, especially in the stomach, that in one or two cases falling under my notice, suspicion of poisoning has been raised. If the disease continues for any length of time, the heart becomes changed in structure or size; dilatation, with general venous engorgement, may ensue, or the cavities may lessen, and be proportioned to the general deficit of blood in the whole system. At times, from the uncontractile condition of the right side of the heart, the venous accumulation is so excessive, that the frontal veins start like whip-cords, on the surface; whilst serous effusion pours into the ventricles of the brain, followed by more or less strabismus. Or other errors of motion or of sensation ensue, their permanency depending on the heart's condition and its capacity to react ; or on the structural changes of the brain, softening of its substance not being an uncommon attendant. The colliquative diarrhœa, so frequent an attendant on the latter stages of consumption, is not always to be regarded as the *cause* of the rapid waste of strength, and lowering of the resisting power of the patient. Many times the diarrhœa is the mere index that waste *has* taken place. It tells that the organic forces of the system are too rapidly expending; that a species of putrescence has commenced in the structures, and in their albuminous supplies, which should have had vital resistance to perform their part longer; it proclaims too truly, that the breach is greater than the repair, and that the bridge of life is trembling and crumbling under the hastening footsteps of the self-armed soldiers of death. If these panic-bearers, these debauched partisans in the ranks of life, find no discharge, the contagion of their retention increases, and all resistance is broken down. Thus it is that the diarrhœa, so dreaded in phthisis, may become preservative under proper management.

Nor are "chronic diarrhœas," at times, to be viewed in any other light. They may be preservative, although they may be exhausting; but exhaustion is better than death. The over-rapid waste of decaying structures must find an exit, if possible. The proper intestinal glands are called upon for excretive function. The hand of God placed these glands in their proper place, and endowed them with their depurating power; yet, His writing is ignored by some of the late fatuists in medicine; and the pent-up impurities from tissues, whose type-life has been spent, are allowed to collect in the blood, poisoning the very founts of recuperative effort.

From these views, a philosophy in treatment can be garnered. The *real* efficiency of remedies is to be seen. Astringents, as tannin, catechu, kino, &c., act by their chemico-mechanical properties of constricting the glandular exits. The propriety of their administration depends whether the irritation of these organs establish the severe drain on the system, or whether these glands perform their legitimate functions, in giving exit to these poisonous products of internal tissue waste. And the cause of the waste itself is also to be considered. It may be from the too rapid exercise of the reproductive forces, loading the blood with the debris of portions no longer useful, (and this is very rare;) or, it may result from their inefficiency, whereby the blood becomes surcharged with the blasted cells of abortive renewal. And this latter condition is frequent. Then, kino, nor tannin, nor any other astringent, is needed; but those remedies having organic, restraining, or supporting properties, are to be depended on. Not with the view of arresting the diarrhœa itself, but of *retarding the necessity* for tissue supply, and affording time proportionate to the inactivity of the remodeling power. Hence, opium does not act by any property of astringency in these cases; but through its organic, restrictive, or paralyzing power, by which the reproductive interchanges are modified. The same may be said of sugar of lead; it is an organic paralyzer, independent of its chemical action over the fluids.

Space is not given for further illustrations of these philosophies of treatment; the hint is sufficient. It is only through similar views that the obstructed streams of medicine can be permanently opened into the sea of science. Whenever this takes place, even the adventurous empiricist will be borne more safely upon the tide that sweeps through the true channel. The present disgraceful bandying of "pathies," whether Homœopathy, or its so-nicknamed Allopathy, will not serve to arm men—(and some of them really clever men on both sides)— against each other, to the detriment of their self-respect, of science, and of their patients particularly. These contendings must sooner or later be harmonized, under the one flag of "rationalistic" medicine. Truth is gained by the study of nature, and not by creating a primer for her, with fables which have their sole foundation in imagination, and their belief in infancy or ignorance.

It may not be out of place to mention, that some forms of diarrhœa (more or less chronic) depend upon malarial poisoning of the blood, or perhaps more truly, of the nervous centres. The organic forces become deranged, and the blood is surcharged with the products of decomposition, or of retardation, to a vast amount. Diarrhœa becomes significant of the fact merely, but is not the disease. The amount of the poison is so great, or its power to impress the nervous system so violent and prostrative, that the blood may be arrested in its *own* renewals, or the structures may be lowered in their power to assimilate their normal constituents. Pallor, loss of flesh, and diarrhœa evidence these conditions, the latter being frequently preservative; or if not attending, life may be paralyzed in the cold grasp of death, with symptoms of uræmic or other blood-poisoning, from the retention of so much animal impurity. Although opium may retard tissue waste, or sugar of lead act in its twofold capacity of restraining organic activity, and constringing the outlets, still the zymotic cause has to be recognized; and quinine, chinoidine, and even arsenic, &c., have to be conjoined to effect a cure. Here the endermic application of these remedies over the spinal tract will serve most important ends. In almost all of these cases, the elaboration of albumen is excessive or imperfect: early decay is impregnated with it, and the tissues so formed have their early type-limit impressed on them. They soon decay, loading to excess the overburdened blood. Cannot the value of the peculiar properties of arsenic, of bichloride of mercury, and other remedies of this class, be seen; when their influence in *rendering the albumen less impressible*, and probably the evolution fibrin more perfect, is daily witnessed, not only in the living, but also in the dead structures? Do not certain surgeons practically find the value of these remedies, and style them, in minute doses, as tonics, in the leuco-phlegmatic or albumino-scrofulous? Is not the reason plain? And thus it is that, in proper cases, arsenic in minute doses becomes a life-giver; whilst in larger doses it is a destroyer, whose footsteps may be rapid or slow, and against whom the very tissues themselves are preserved as witnesses! It may open the door to death, but keeps back its dismal companion, decay.

We have already overrun our allotted space; but as the object of this paper was not to rehash views already promulgated, nor to re-copy treatments tried, and found useful or useless, we have dilated on the physiological and pathological positions necessary to establish the grounds for a somewhat novel and apparently more rational application of remedial measures. It would seem reasonable that the internal administration of drugs has but a doubtful chance of reaching the ends desired, when the disturbances of the digestive organs are so great. The return to sound action in them must necessarily consume time, and time is not to be lost as regards the changes progressing in the chest. These are to be modified by such *direct* means as lie within our power—not through the route of the stomach and intestines—but through their superficies, and by local absorptional application to the laryngeal and bronchial membranes themselves.

When the errors of assimilation are either not great, or are those of impediment more than of destructive impairment, then the internal administration of remedial measures may be trustily conjoined. Many times the difficulties of the digestive organs are engrafted on deficiencies of arterialization from a disturbed condition of the lungs; and these cases certainly are not to be remedied by measures directed to the stomach, liver, or bowels. The defects within the chest are to be locally attended to, and the gastro-intestinal membranes are to be *kept for the purposes of nourishment*, and not for those of medication. Their restitution progresses with the benefits accruing in the lungs.

The same is seen in the easily examined disorders of the larynx and pharynx. Follicular depravities take place, and although they might be associated with disturbed gastric functions, still, the influence of the diseased secretions poured out by these glands upon the gastric membrane, or on the gastric juice, is such, that healthy digestion is destroyed, and the consecutive derangements arising from this induced condition are but too frequently viewed as the causes of the subjective disorder. But the fallacy of such a view is to be exposed, by the return to health being effected by topical medication to the diseased surfaces, without a drop of medicine being swallowed. The cases of the so-called consumption of the larnyx, for the most part, commence in this way. In the previously healthy, tubercule may result from these digestive depreciations. In the scrofulous or blood disordered, the proclivity to its exhibition is hastened. The depositions of tubercle are within the lung, rarely in the larnyx, although tuberculous degeneration may ensue in the small bronchial tubes.

Some of the most aggravated cases of dyspepsia falling under my care have been entirely recovered by topical application to the throat surfaces. The ulcerations of the bronchial and exposed lung tissues are likewise amenable to local treatments, and their vast superficial expansion is to be employed for remedial purposes. Blood changes, diseases, nervous impressibilities, whether sedative or stimulant, are daily witnessed from the inhalation of zymotic vapors, mephitic or anæsthetic gases; whilst the pure air of the prairie, or the chlorinated breezes from the sea, find their life-invigorating powers through the extended surfaces of respiration. An outward ulcer may be cured by internal administration of blood alteratives, when dependent on a constitutional affection; but a simple ulcer, originating by accident, or from some local imperfection of the remodeling process, is readily healed by direct application. You may attract the attention of a patient by internal remedies, but you cure the ulcer by local applications.

The analysis of the tissue of the lung differs somewhat from that of muscle, inasmuch, that it affords oleic and margaric acids free and in combination with soda, and cerebric, or oleo-phosphoric acid, with a notable amount of cholesterine. The analysis of tubercle resembles that afforded by the parenchyma of the lung, excepting certain differences of proportion in the component principles. Chloride of sodium particularly is in excess in tuberculous matter, whilst the phosphate of lime is much smaller, (that is, in unchanged tubercle.) The amount of cholesterine by weight in tubercle is at least ten times greater than in healthy lung tissue. It is somewhat singular that an excess of this product should be found in so many grave diseases. Whether this substance, so rich in calorifiant principles—carbon and hydrogen—forms a cause of the deposition of tubercle, or whether it is merely retained, and accumulates by disengagement, from the blood supplying it normally to the tissues that have wasted or been metamorphosed, cannot now be discussed. It is worthy of remark, however, that this remarkable substance is also found in large excess in fatty liver, the so frequent attendant of pulmonary consumption. It mostly presents itself whenever oxygenation is deficient. But whether it collects because of the loss of the normal supply of oxygen, or whether it abounds in undue amount in the blood, even if the quantity of oxygen is normally afforded, are questions for further investigation. Generally, it is indicative of waste of brain and nerve tissue.

The analysis of tubercle differs in itself, according to its state, but not according to its situation. Certain modifications ensue between crude, cheesy, softened, and concreting tubercles. In crude tubercle, according to Boudet, the casein exists chiefly in an insoluble state, whilst in softened tubercle the casein is soluble from the developed alkali. In fatty liver the saponifiable fats may be found twenty times greater in quantity than in the sound state, whilst the natural tissue falls to one-half its normal weight, attended with an enormous excess of cholesterine.

The length of this paper has already extended beyond the limits allowed. The physiological and pathological conditions have been sufficiently dwelt upon to indicate not only the basis of treatments, but the causes for the inadequacy so generally attending the administration of remedies. I have now only space to call the attention of the profession to those rational views as regards the eradication of the tuberculous dyscrasia, and the process of affording to the diseased lung those *nutrient elements which constitute their tissue in health, and which are defective or deficient in tubercular ravages.* These desired results are to be effected by internal administration through the digestive organs, and by inhalation, or direct absorption, or contact of the remedial and nutrient substances by the mucous membrane of the larynx and bronchial tubes, in conjunction with applications to the surface of the chest and abdomen. Nor are the nutrient elements alone to be afforded by direct inhalation; but those volatile remedial substances can be applied to the affected surfaces, together with liquid preparations gradually introduced within the cavity of the larynx, after tolerance has been established. The value attached to many fatty ointments is owing, in many instances, to the absolute nourishment afforded to the diseased surfaces, as the preparations mingled with the oily substances are sometimes inert or not absorbed.

The exclusion of air from the surface of course has to be taken into consideration. Glycerine, independent of any other influence, becomes a valuable nutrient application to the ulcerous parts. Through frictional applications of nutrient substances, to the surface of the chest and abdomen, life has been supported in many exhausting diseases; and also, where there has been structural impediment to internal digestion. Cod-liver oil, diligently rubbed in, has proved in my hands, and in others, a most reliable method of support, and a means of affording to the blood and tissues the oleaginous materials so imperatively demanded in diseases of the lungs, mesenteric glands, &c. The stomach may have refused the administration of oils, or, from duodenal derangements, their absorption by the lacteals could not be attained, whereby the *enfilming* of the chyle corpuscle was arrested or rendered imperfect. In such cases the endermic method must be adopted, and will generally be found beneficial. By the direct inhalatory application of the volatile fatty matters, the exudative depositions of albumino-tuberculous matter within the air-cells are rendered in a condition more ready to be reabsorbed, or assimilated. By the vehicle of vapor, or of spray, the substances entering not only into the composition of the lung and tissues of the blood, can be directly applied, but those preparations having a specific remedial purpose can be introduced. A great desideratum is also obtained by these methods—the stomach and whole intestinal tract is reserved for nutriment, and not deranged by uncertain medication. At all events, the internal administration of remedial agents can be lessened to tolerance, when the digestive organs are themselves disordered; whilst their labor for self-restoration is not impeded, or so much impaired, and the affected lung tissues lose no time in their acts of recuperation.

Climate-change for the consumptive has killed as many as it has cured. "To the South," has been the watchword cry. But the South is not all sunny and balmy. It, too, has its bleak, dry, or damp alternations. It has its oppressive days and its fitful night changes. Caution is lost sight of by the hoping patient. He is in the South, and what need is there for prudence? He leaves comforts in exchange for the mere necessaries of life; and is forced upon greater restriction as regards diet, excepting, perhaps, that of fruits. The social relations of home are broken up, or interfered with. There is more necessity for exertion, although indulgence is sought after; and though more rest may be obtained, there is less repose. Besides these drawbacks, there is an everlasting consciousness that he is there for health. From night till morning his cough and his complainings are re-echoed from some adjoining room or house, or reiterated by his like afflicted neighbor. For bronchitic cases, *where the nervous tension is too high*, the change to a warm climate will prove beneficial; but for the opposite conditions of relaxation and anæmic respiration, the rarefied and warmer air adds to the distress. There is a difference, also, as regards the wastage of moisture by the lung. Some exhale an enormous amount of vapor, whilst others throw off but little. In the former a warm, moist climate would serve to arrest the exhalation, whilst a dry, cold climate must tend to increase it. In the latter, the opposite results obtain. From practical experience, this difference between dry or moist atmosphere is known by the patient; and if not known, it can readily be made manifest, by experiment. As a general rule, I am more in the habit of advising tuberculous patients, requiring change, to seek a dry, uniform, northern climate, and especially if they require or find oleaginous substances to agree with them. In the southern latitudes, these oil matters, so essential with many, do not agree so well. The respiration is less frequent and deep; the relaxation extends to the remodeling process, and although the decay of tissue may be retarded, yet the *rebuilding* of healthy structure does not progress. Even *cream*, which stands next to cod-liver oil as a tissue regenerator, cannot be well borne. With these, the warm vapors from the sugar-house agree best. *Their application is direct to the bronchial surfaces.* Many incur chills, and these are laid at the door of malarial infection. But, in reality, the chills are more often the precursors or attendants of tubercular softening, or of progressive structural declension. The table-lands of Mexico probably form the most healthful resort for the consumptive.

Remedies that restrain tissue waste, by affording to the inspired oxygen, carbon, hydrogen, or nitrogen, are valuable auxiliaries in the

3

eradication or cure of tubercular phthisis. Hence tea, coffee, cream, &c., find advocates for their use. Other remedies, as arsenic, corrosive sublimate, creosote, naphtha, &c., that have the property of impressing upon albumen and its compounds a state of resistance to abnormal decay, become, in skillful hands, powerful abettors in restraining waste, and in promoting recuperative repair of tissue. Opium has also its place; its abuse should suggest its use. It becomes, under scientific direction, a boon, and not a bane. Its power to control the *necessity* for tissue supply, by restraining the activity of the assimilative processes; its stimulant effect, in certain doses, over the nerves of organic life; its secondary actions in producing cerebral congestion, by which not only the due pressure is maintained within the brain, when needed from anæmia, but by which rest may be obtained for its wearied functions;—these, and other benefits, give to opium a place of trust in the hands of the skilled rationalistic physician, unequaled by any other drug, but which are daily abused by ignorant empiricists, or the routine practitioner. Alcohol, in shape of brandy, rum, or whiskey, has its uses; the lungs of tuberculous drunkards proclaim in favor of its use, but not of its abuse. Both free carbon and hydrogen are afforded, in place of the elements of the wasting tissues being consumed by the inspired oxygen; whilst the albumen compounds are rendered less liable to premature putrescence. Whiskey from corn, or the Bourbon whiskey, is decidedly the best form of remedial supply, the contained fusil oil having a beneficial influence. Wines, containing a due proportion of alcohol, with phosphoric matter combined with lime, potash, &c., are also vehicles of support and recuperation; and especially during the disposition to the calcareous metamorphosis of tubercle, in which the phosphate and carbonate of lime, with more or less silex, and oxide of iron, play so notable a part. Certain spring waters, holding in solution the above elements, as the Lebanon Spring water, have been found beneficial in this condition. Their inhalation will serve a better purpose towards local assimilation. The soluble salts, as the chloride of sodium, phosphate and sulphate of soda, are also portions of these concretions. The incineration of tubercle, on analysis, corresponds remarkably with that of the concretions.

The object of this paper is not to rehearse treatments already tried. Their road is known, and too well beaten. But it is to direct attention to a path whose windings have been only partially explored; and to explain, on the basis of rational science, the indications for remedial action, and to classify the agents with the ends desired—the how and the wherefore of modern therapeutics. We have not, then, redressed the meagre skeletons of wasted treatments, and flaunted them under their dominos before the world, nor embodied those palliatives so familiar to the profession, and so daily employed by the people. But the object has been to disrobe that scourge " to one-third of mankind" of its artificial terrors and its mysteries, that it should stand naked before all, that its make and proportions should be known. To do this, its footsteps of stealthy approach had to be traced through all the great avenues of life. Its dwelling-house within the chest had to be entered, where the robberies of the blood were deposited; or where, invited by other evil companions, it left the proceeds of its ravages, amidst the wreck of all that once was sound, but now tenanted by wasteful marauders. It has been shown that Life, sitting on its throne of harmonious organic relation, could find itself quietly or quickly undermined by the sappers, which might deposit their grains of destruction, or boldly issue forth, and cut off supply after supply, till the white flag of starvation was the only one of peace. It was also shown, that not through the broad conduits of renewal alone was this demon of human destruction to be tracked; but that, through the electric influences of the nervous system, impressions were conveyed, which caused the grief-bowed to bend yet more, or else made purity a battening residence of a vicious spirit, which left naught but blighted remains to tell of its vampire course.

From all this degradation a practical moral arose. It taught that early principles should be attended to; that the very organic alphabet in the mouth should be watched, lest an early error should ensue. How changes may be engrafted here and there, in the various passages of life, and the "cell," whose office it is to bear renewal and similitude to every portion of the body, should enfilm itself with delicate oil, that the lamp of life might be replenished, dispensing heat and renewed invitation to the chambers of the chest. It told how nature craved supply from the outer world, when the blood could not fulfill its function.

In summing up, we find:

1. That pulmonary consumption may be a disease originating in the blood; or in the tissue of the lung itself; or from deranged nervous actions.

2. That tubercle is a product, the witness of blasted "cell growth," originating from the imperfection of the nutrient materials; or from a disturbed elective action inherent to the tissues themselves.

3. That ravages similar to those effected by the pressure and offence of tubercle, may ensue, without being caused by the evolution of, although attended with, tubercle, in portions more or less distant.

4. That structural changes arise from the abnormal influences of the nervous system.

5. That in some phthisis is hereditary, and in others is self-induced.

6. That it may waste every fat-cell, without great attendant loss of strength; whilst at other times, fat is not so entirely consumed, as muscular fibre is degenerated, and rendered less contractile.

7. That it accompanies or alternates with fatty degeneration of the liver, and of other organs.

8. That it may be incurrent with albuminuria, diabetes, or that the eruptive diseases may be its developing point.

9. That pregnancy may afford a certain arrest in its progressive ravages; or, by increasing the albuminous composition of the blood, the liability to certain tuberculous dyscrasia might be rendered greater.

10. That the "colliquative" diarrhœa, attending tubercular phthisis, may be preservative.

11. That the enfilming with oil of the true chyle corpuscle is a most important step towards future assimilation.

12. That follicular laryngeal disease may be at the bottom of tubercular degenerations and disorders of the digestive system.

13. That the pulmonary and skin surfaces afford a vast channel for remedial application and nutrient supply.

14. That alcoholic, opiate, arsenical, and other remedies having the power to restrict the disposition to too rapid change or decay in the albuminous products, are required.

15. That, to have normal blood products, the chyle formations must be healthily sustained.

16. That the selection of dry or moist climates depends on the amount of vapor exhaled or retained by the patient.

791 BROADWAY.

ERRATA.

Page 6, line 6 from bottom, read. *by which*, instead of whereby.
" 11, " 11 " top, " *barely sufficient*, instead of sufficient barely.
" 21, " 12 " bottom, " increased *cardiac* irritability, instead of increased irritability.
" 28, " 18 " top, " *an* early type limit, instead of their early, &c.
" 28, " 22 " " " evolution *of* fibrin, instead of evolution fibrin.

[From the American Medical Monthly for June, 1859.]